MANVILLE BRANCH
W9-ALJ-402

ONE WIDE RIVER TO CROSS

ONE WIDE RIVER TO CROSS

Adapted by BARBARA EMBERLEY Illustrated by ED EMBERLEY

Old Noah built himself an ark,

He built it out of hick'ry bark.

The animals came in one by one,

And Japheth played the big bass drum.

The animals came in two by two,

The alligator lost his shoe.

The animals came in three by three,

The ostrich and the chickadee.

The animals came in four by four,

The hippopotamus blocked the door.

The animals came in five by five,

The yak in slippers did arrive.

The animals came in six by six,

The elephants were doing tricks.

The animals came in seven by seven,

A drop of rain dropped out of heaven.

The animals came in eight by eight,

Some came in by roller skate.

The animals came in nine by nine,

The cats and kittens kept in line.

The animals came in ten by ten,

Let’s go back and start again.

One wide river, and that wide river is Jordan,

One wide river, there's one wide river to cross.

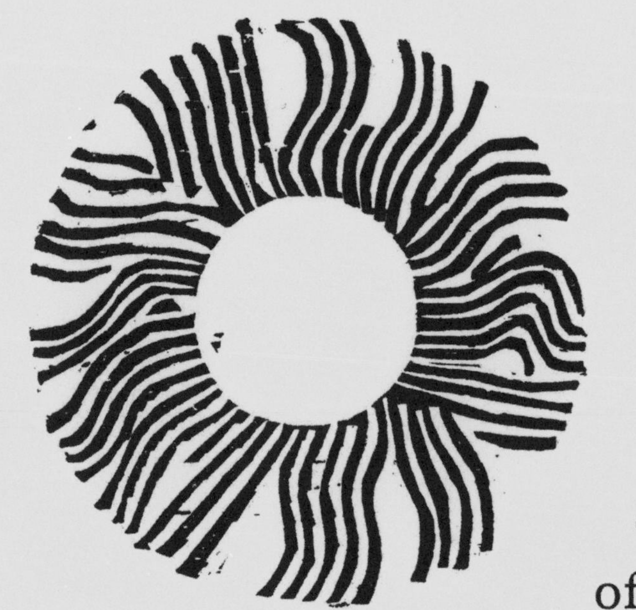

It rained and rained and
rained till the high hills and all
the mountains were covered.
The waters receded and the ark
came to rest on the mountains
of Ararat. To show that He
would never again send such a
flood, God set a rainbow in the sky.

ONE WIDE RIVER TO CROSS

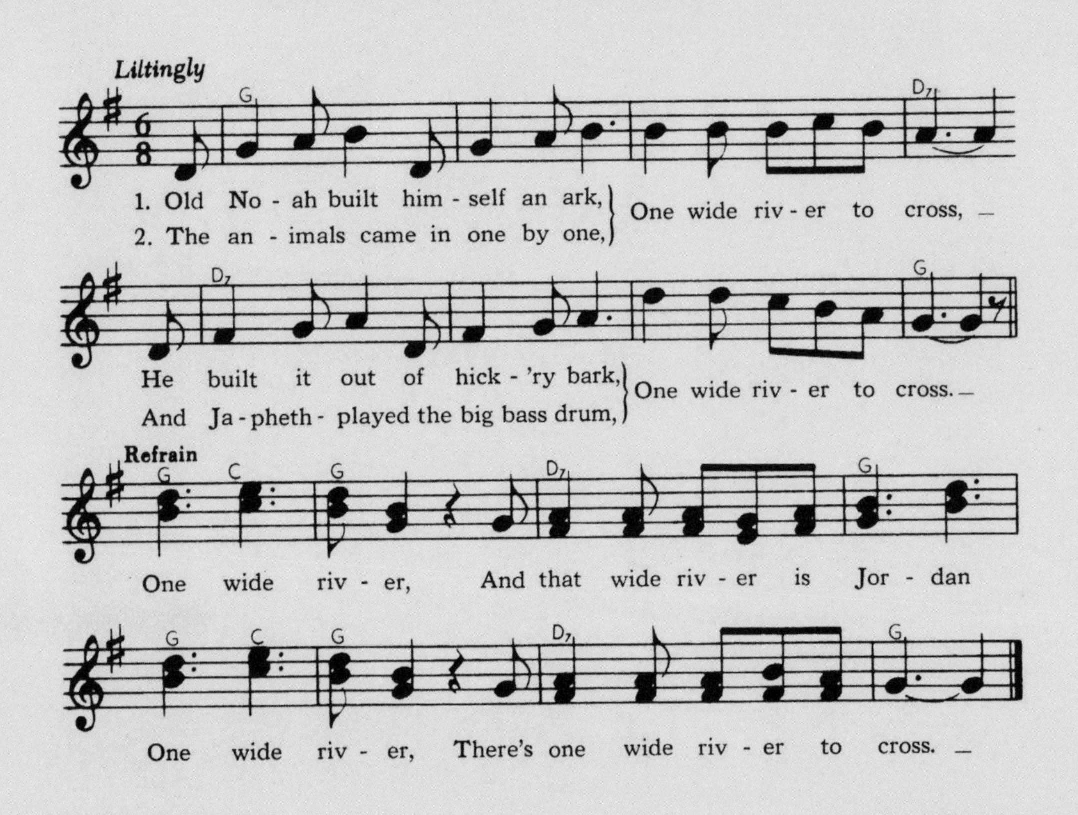

3. The animals came in two by two, one wide river to cross,
   The alligator lost his shoe, one wide river to cross.

   REFRAIN:
   One wide river, and that wide river is Jordan,
   One wide river, there's one wide river to cross.

4. The animals came in three by three, one wide river to cross,
   The ostrich and the chickadee, one wide river to cross.
   (Refrain)

5. The animals came in four by four, one wide river to cross,
   The hippopotamus blocked the door, one wide river to cross.
   (Refrain)

6. The animals came in five by five, one wide river to cross,
   The yak in slippers did arrive, one wide river to cross.
   (Refrain)

7. The animals came in six by six, one wide river to cross,
   The elephants were doing tricks, one wide river to cross.
   (Refrain)

8. The animals came in seven by seven, one wide river to cross,
   A drop of rain dropped out of heaven, one wide river to cross.
   (Refrain)

9. The animals came in eight by eight, one wide river to cross,
   Some came in by roller skate, one wide river to cross.
   (Refrain)

10. The animals came in nine by nine, one wide river to cross,
    The cats and kittens kept in line, one wide river to cross.
    (Refrain)

11. The animals came in ten by ten, one wide river to cross,
    Let's go back and start again, one wide river to cross.
    (Refrain)

One Wide River to Cross
Adapted by Barbara Emberley
Illustrated by Ed Emberley

First Published, 1966
First AMMO Books Edition, 2014
Acquisitions Editor: Gloria Fowler
Production: Megan Shoemaker
Copy Edit: Sara Richmond
Thank you: Rebecca Emberley
ISBN: 9781623260590
Library of Congress Control Number: 2014939830

Printed in China.

Note:

The first page shows Shem, one of Noah's three sons. On the third page is the raven which Noah sent out to see if the flood had ended. On the sixth and seventh pages, Noah's son Japheth plays the drum and Ham plays the horn. The animals are, from left to right, the basilisk, the unicorn, the manticore, the griffin.